Rogue Dentist

© Robert Scott 2024

Contents.

Synopsis.

"Rogue Dentist" is a short story based on my personal relationship I had with my dentist during the early 90s.

The story centres around the economic climate at the time, and how the dentist felt betrayed by his bank manager. The dentist embarks on a mission of revenge to get back at the bank manager and ruin him forever.

Chapter 1 : Terry Sleeman

Because of the nature of this true story, my lawyer advised me to change the names of everyone involved, even if all the characters have long since passed away.

"Don't risk it Rob for Christ's sake! I'm still dealing with all the crap from the last story you wrote."

"Don't worry Jerry, I won't fuck up like last time, I promise you." I said rather sheepishly. Jerry was rubbing the sides of his chubby, fat head, his tortoiseshell rimmed glasses perched on top, he always did this when he felt stressed out. I always had a job to try my hardest not to smirk as he did this.

Jerry Goldbird had been my lawyer ever since my ex-wife tried to take me to the cleaners all those years ago, without Jerry's help back then, I'd probably still be in the shit now. He wasn't the cheapest lawyer, but like with all things in life; you get what you pay for.

Let me take you back to the 16th of September 1992, often referred to as "Black Wednesday". The UK government finally left the ERM (exchange rate mechanism) and the Pound devalued 20% - showing how much it was overvalued. In Sptember 1992, interest rates were 10%, despite the economy being in recession. The government even increased rates further to 12%, and even temporarily to 15%, in an effort to protect the value of Sterling.

Such high interest rates were obviously unsustainable, which subsequently made mortgage payments very expensive, and many homeowners saw a fall in disposable income leading to lower spending. The bottom subsequently dropped out of the housing market like an obese lady who has a double prolapse whilst running for the bus, (whilst working in a private medical insurance call centre when I was in my twenties, I received a phone call from a client who had actually experienced something so horrendous), but that's another story which I won't go into right now.

So now I've given you a brief rundown of the economic climate at the time, let me get back to the story.

Terry Sleeman was my dentist back then in the early 90s, a brilliant dentist it must be said, you could say he had a gift. He had a way with people that I've never seen before or since; it didn't matter if the patients were young or elderly. He always knew how to gauge people quickly, and he had the knack of making them feel at ease and would always leave people in a better mood than he found them.

I first met Terry when I got a job running a large antiques shop two doors down from his dental surgery. The owner of the antiques shop was a sweet, little old lady named Bunty Venison. Bunty had had an amazing life, she'd spent most of her life out in India during the days of the Raj with her husband who was a brigadier in the British army, stationed up in the Khyber Pass in the Hindu Kush. They both returned to England after the second World War, and shortly afterwards in the early 50s, the brigadier retired to pursue his lifelong hobby, sailing, and drinking. Their marriage came to an abrupt end in the late 60s when the brigadier ran off with the housekeeper, it turned out they'd been having an affair for years, and so, Bunty kept the vast country house high up in the outskirts of the village. The brigadier had a new house built for himself and his lover down by the river, to be closer to his beloved 50 foot schooner. I first met Bunty by chance, as I was walking my dog along the road at the bottom of the long driveway that led up to her house. She was walking down the driveway towards me with her two black labradors, Rakesh and Tamila, named after the last two man servants she had employed out in India. We hit it off straight away, as we are both animal lovers. She invited me up to the house later that afternoon for high tea. I had no idea what high tea was, images of huge pots of tea laced with magic mushrooms & cannabis indica came to mind. I returned to the large Victorian house at the top of the hill later that day at four in the afternoon as requested. As I entered the vast porch area in front of the huge door, I could see all around me museum style display cabinets housing a vast array of stuffed, wild animals, in varying poses in woodland settings. There was everything from foxes, stoats and badgers, and even some creatures I'd never seen before. As I was inspecting the stuffed animals on display, the door swung open, and Bunty invited me into the kitchen to sit down. I took a seat at the impressively large oak table, and could see a vast quantity of little cakes and sandwiches neatly arranged at one end of the table where the only two chairs were. The interior of the house was a bit of a wreck, it was plain to see there were no more servants or maids employed there.

Bunty placed an old-fashioned, porcelain teapot on the table and sat down at the chair at the head of the table next to me. She began to tell me her life story in great detail as she poured the tea; I picked up my dainty cup and saucer to smell the tea, it didn't smell like mushrooms or cannabis, I let out a sigh of relief and said politely "Darjeeling! super!"

"I couldn't agree more Robert, it's all I drink these days, that and the occasional gin & tonic on special occasions." replied Bunty as she offered me the plate of cucumber sandwiches cut into little triangles.

We chatted for well over an hour and Bunty eventually got onto the subject of her poor health, she'd had two hip replacements and said she could barely make the long walk down to the village anymore to go to her antiques shop. She asked me if I knew anyone that would like to take over the running of the shop for her, as she didn't want to sell it. I told her that as I was currently between jobs and had a lot of time on my hands at the moment; so I said I would be delighted to give it a go.

"Oh how wonderful Robert, I'm so glad you can help me, heres the key to the shop and heres my telephone number, in case you need to contact me for anything." She said as she handed me a large key with her phone number written on a scrap of paper.

"You can start on Monday if you like?" Bunty said as she stood up to show me out.

"I can't wait Bunty, I'm really looking forward to it, I love antiques and old treasures." I said as I opened the heavy door to go back out onto the porch. She told me again to call her if I needed anything and wished me a good afternoon, and that was how I got the job running Bunty's antique shop near the dental surgery in the village.

Terry Sleeman wasn't just my dentist but also a very good friend, we would often meet up for drinks at our local pub after work, and go sailing on the weekends in the local regattas and races.

We were both members of the same Rotary Club and Freemasons Lodge in Plymouth. Terry was the one that got me into the Freemasons, although I didn't climb the ladder very high unlike him, because I always had trouble with reciting the lengthy passages required for the ceremonies and rituals. To be honest with you, I really enjoyed the social side of things more, and the lunches & dinners we had there had always been first rate, better than most top class restaurants.

For me, Terry was the ultimate family man with a lovely wife called Barbera and seven kids in tow. They were both on their second marriage (something I vowed I would never to do again) with Terry having three kids from his first marriage and Barbera had two from her previous. When they got together, they thought it would be a good idea to have another two; I thought they were stark raving mad but I guess some people just like a really busy, noisy household.

In the early summer of 1992 they moved house because they needed something bigger, understandable when you've got such a big family, seven kids ranging from the ages of two to 17, hectic. They had two Volvo estate cars and Terry was also an avid motorcycle enthusiast; he rode a Kawasaki ZX-10 to work when it wasn't raining and one time he gave me a lift home on it when my car wouldn't start. I only went on the back of it with him once, because on the way home Terry thought it would be funny to open it right up going down the dual carriageway, the ZX-10 was the fastest, road legal production bike at the time with a claimed top speed of 178 miles per hour right out of the box. I required a shower and a change of trousers when I got home.

Chapter 2 : The bank manager

Terry was at home on the 16th of September 1992, the kids were in bed and both parents were in the lounge watching the 9 o'clock news. The big, headline story was all about the recession and "Black Wednesday" (the phrase was used about 20 times in 5 minutes), and the impending doom that homeowners were going to experience. You can imagine the look of horror on Terry & Barbera's face, they had recently purchased a new house and within a few months, they found themselves in negative equity and interest rates had gone through the roof. They were both pretty good with money but because of the size of their family, and having two of their kids in private schools, their overheads were a lot higher than the average family.

The next day after work I met Terry in the Dog & Duck pub as usual. I got there first as I'd bunked off work early. I ordered myself a pint of Guinness and sat down in my favourite spot to read the local rag, an hour went by and still no Terry. I thought this rather odd as Terry was never late, especially when it came to after-work drinks.

He eventually turned up just after seven thirty, by which time I was already halfway down my third pint. He walked up to the bar with a very solemn look on his face, something I'd never seen before.

"Large brandy please Sally", he said to the barmaid. It was plain to see he was pretty stressed out and not in the mood for the usual chit-chat that he normally did with bar staff.

"Bad day at the office Terry?" Sally said with genuine concern on her face as she'd only ever seen him in a jovial mood.

"Don't ask." Terry said, and picked up his glass and came and took a seat at the table where I was reading the paper.

"What's up Terry?, you look like you've seen a ghost." I said as I finished my pint and gestured to Sally to bring me another.

"Did you watch the news last night Rob?" Terry asked with a look of despair on his face.

"Of course I bloody didn't, I never watch the news, all doom & gloom, never a happy story."

"Well, the shits really hit the fan now." Terry said staring into his brandy glass.

Terry explained to me the current economic situation, and how he was going to be in serious trouble financially when the new interest rates kicked in. The interest rates were already high before "Black Wednesday", but now it was all going to get a lot worse.

I was lucky that I was renting at the time so this sort of thing didn't really affect me, but I felt genuinely sorry for those that had recently bought houses.

"I'm already in my overdraft every month and now this has happened, christ knows how I'm gonna get myself out of this shitstorm." Terry said, and I could see his right leg was shaking under the table as he was talking to me.

I told Terry to not believe everything he sees on tv and in the papers, and ordered him another large brandy; I said to give it a few weeks and everything will probably calm down.

"God, I hope so Rob." Terry said as he took another sip of brandy.

I managed to change the topic of conversation, and we got onto the subject of sailing as there was a race coming up later on that month.

we ended up chatting for another hour before we both paid our slates and went home.

I saw little of Terry the rest of September and October, as he was working his bollocks off every day in his surgery till gone 8 o'clock most evenings. He didn't even call into the pub for a few beers after work anymore as he was trying to save every penny he had.

The next time I saw Terry was the beginning of November because the yacht race got cancelled because of foul weather. I had a terrible toothache one evening and phoned Terry explaining the agony I was in. He always had a small make-shift surgery at home so he could take patients in emergencies after hours, he told me to come round straight away, which I did.

After the offending tooth got pulled out with very little fuss, we were both in the kitchen chatting away over a glass of scotch, before long he started talking about the fact that he was going further and further into debt because of the skyrocketing interest rates.

"Why don't you get an appointment with the bank manager?, ask him to extend your overdraft, or maybe he can do a short-term loan or something." I said.

"Already have done, got an appointment first thing tomorrow morning." Terry said as he poured us both another whisky.

Both Terry & I had the same bank manager at the Plymouth city centre branch of Lloyds Bank. Terry had always got on pretty well with him, and had even seconded his proposal into the Freemasons like me. To be honest, I didn't like the guy that much, I could tolerate him in small doses but that was about it. I probably didn't earn enough money for him to be nice to me, plus the fact that he knew I hated bankers & politicians and the like. Nigel Jenkins was his name, I thought he looked like a weasel. He had horrible ratty, brown, nicotine-stained teeth and always wore terrible suits, he looked more like a failed geography teacher than a bank manager.

Unfortunately, the appointment didn't go well for Terry. Nigel refused to extend his overdraft and wouldn't give him a short-term loan either. Nigel said, that because of the current economic climate his hands were tied and there was nothing he could do. Not long after the unsuccessful rendezvous with Nigel Jenkins, Terry found out from a fellow Freemason that Nigel had been shouting his mouth off to fellow Freemasons, about how Terry was in the shit financially, and would more than likely go bust before long. Apparently Jenkins seemed to think it was funny (what a sick bastard I thought, this is why I hate bankers). Upon hearing this ghastly revelation, Terry hit the roof, he was livid as you can imagine. He could sort of half understand why he'd been turned down for a loan etc etc and for whatever reasons, but to tell everyone else about it was unforgivable.

Terry recounted all this to me a few days later when we were down the snooker hall one evening after work, I couldn't believe what I was being told.

"What an evil bugger." I said to Terry as I missed another easy red. I was rubbish at snooker, I much preferred playing nine ball American pool, I didn't have the patience for snooker as the frames took too long. Terry took his shot, a fairly tricky pot, but as always it went straight in as my head went down inspecting the state of my worn-out shoes.

"We need to teach that arsehole Jenkins a lesson." I said, as Terry continued to pot another ball. I was bang up for a solution requiring violence, but Terry just shook his head and said it wouldn't solve anything, we'd only get in trouble with the law and be no better off. Terry was right, but me being me I wouldn't let it go.

"Theres got to be something we can do, can't let him get away with it, it can't be right!" I exclaimed whilst chalking my cue.

Terry was a total pacifist, I don't think he'd ever been in a proper fistfight in his life, never once had he raised his fists in anger. He was way too smart for that sort of thing.

"I'm gonna destroy him, not with my hands but with my intellect, that fucker will regret the day he ever met me." Terry said as he walked round the table to finish his pint of bitter.

Chapter 3 : The plan

Terry was in his study at home on his computer, printing out paperwork for the Rotary club, he was club secretary and one of the few people in the club who knew anything about computers. All he could think about was how to get back at Jenkins for his betrayal.

Whilst loading up the printer with another wad of A4 paper, it came to him like a lightning bolt in the brain.

"That's it, I've got it, fucking yes!" he said to himself, as he sat down again in his tired old leather office chair. The best way to hurt a banker is financially, all they care about is money after all, they certainly don't give two shits about people.

Terry set to work on his new plan, he was already feeling better about everything. The next morning before work, Terry went into the town centre to one of those places where you can have a post box to get mail delivered to for a small fee. He wrote his name down on the paperwork and handed the form back to the old lady on the desk.

"Pleased to meet you Nigel Jenkins" said the old lady, the neon strip lighting reflecting off her blue rinsed hair.

"I just need a form of I.D. to complete the process." She said to Terry.

"Ah well, the thing is you see, I lost my wallet the other day and I've applied for a new driving license, can I get it sent to this P.O. box? when it turns up, we can complete the paperwork."

"Yes, of course Mr Jenkins that won't be a problem," she replied with a smile on her face.

"I'll pay for the first month upfront in cash as that's all I've got on me right now. I can pop back in when my new cheque book & driving license arrives, then I'll be able to write you a cheque for the whole year's fee." Said Terry.

"Very well Mr Jenkins, that'll work fine." Said the old lady behind the desk as she handed him his key for the mailbox.

Terry skipped off out of the P.O. box place and went to work via the post office. There, he posted a form requesting a provisional driving license, using Nigel Jenkins's name, date of birth and National Insurance number. Terry had all this information because he was the secretary at the Rotary club, and had access to all the club members details. A week went by and he went back to ask if his new provisional driving license had arrived, sure enough it had and he completed the paperwork with the old lady he'd met previously. She asked him if his new cheque book had been delivered but Terry replied "Not yet Mrs Grayson, hopefully next week."

To all the people born after 9/11, I must state that before this catastrophic event happened, things were very different compared to today. There were very few CCTV cameras unlike today, mobile phones were in their infancy and money laundering procedures were pretty much nonexistent. Back in those days, all you needed to open a straightforward chequing account was a form of I.D., such as a driving license or passport, and an address, anyway back to the story.

Terry went home and wrote a letter to the bank, but choosing a different branch to his own. He wrote requesting to open an account in the name of Nigel Jenkins. The first time he'd met Nigel was at the Rotary club during a charity dinner in town. So with all the relevant information mailed to the bank, all Terry had to do now was wait for his new cheque book to be delivered to the P.O. box in the name of Nigel Jenkins.

Another week rolled on by and Terry thought he'd pop into town to see if his, or should I say, "Mr Jenkins's" shiny new Lloyds Bank cheque book had arrived in his newly gained Post Office box. Terry approached the shopfront and as he was about 50 metres away, he could see a van parked outside, with two men wearing brown overalls going in and out, carrying ladders and various tools and huge reels of electrical cable. Terry waited for a few more minutes and could see one of the workers going back to the van again. This time the overall clad worker went back into the premises carrying two large, white security cameras.

"Oh shit!, that's torn it, there could already be some cameras in operation." Terry said to himself standing on the pavement observing from a distance.

"Bugger!, every time I go in there now, my face will be on camera opening the P.O. box."

Terry walked back to where he'd parked the car a few hundred yards away, down a side street off the main road. He sat in his car and thought about what he was going to do.

"How can I go in there without them seeing my face?" he murmured to himself as he turned on the radio for some inspiration. As he was switching stations on the radio, he heard an advert for the motorbike dealership where he'd bought his Kawasaki, saying how they're giving huge discounts on motorcycle helmets. Terry snapped his fingers and started up the car to drive home. He parked the car outside the house and ran straight into the garage, he put on his fullface helmet and gloves and fired up the big 1000 cc machine and screamed off back into town.

It took Terry fifteen minutes to get back into the city centre, he parked the motorbike down another side street a good distance away from the P.O. box place. He then strolled down the high street casually, still with his helmet on. When he was close to the premises, he saw the work van had gone, so he knew the cameras would be in full operation. As he entered the premises, he could see the old lady busy at the front desk with a customer, and there was at least another ten people in there all checking their mail. He nonchalantly breezed in keeping his head down, even though he was still wearing the helmet, and went straight to his mailbox. He turned the key in the slot and sure enough, inside the box, was the envelope from the bank, containing his new cheque book with the standard letter and various other pamphlets you get when you open a new bank account. He snatched the envelope, closed the box and walked straight out, the whole time keeping his head down with no one else taking any notice of him whatsoever. When he got back to the parked motorbike, he realised his hands were shaking ever so slightly. He didn't know if it was because of the excitement or adrenaline, or because he'd done something completely illegal. Anyway, he took off his helmet and walked into the adjacent pub and ordered a half pint of Guinness to settle his nerves. Ten minutes went by as he gently sipped his drink in silence, he paid the landlord and put his helmet back on to walk back to the Bike. He rode home with a big smile on face, grinning from ear to ear, knowing damn well that in his jacket pocket was a real weapon of mass financial destruction. Terry felt just like George Peppard's character "Hannibal Smith", from the popular tv show "The A-Team". As he put the Kawasaki back in the garage and locked the door behind him, he said to himself with a sadistic grin on his face, "I love it when a plan comes together".

Chapter 4 : The magic cheque book

The secret to revenge is very much like the secret to comedy, timing! Christmas was just around the corner and now was the time for Terry Sleeman to put his little plan into action. Terry was wide awake before anyone else in the house, as there was something he needed to do before he got in the shower. Terry quietly tiptoed into the bathroom and locked the door behind him without making a sound. He opened the cabinet above the sink and took out his electric beard trimmer and plugged it into the little, two pin socket on the wall above the sink. For Terry's plan to work he needed to make sure he looked just like that arse of a bank manager Jenkins, so obviously the full beard Terry sported since his mid twenties had to go. Terry had always hated shaving, couldn't see the point as it took too long and always grew back too quickly. He did the bulk of "deforestation" with the little electric device and put it back in the cabinet. He rummaged about looking for some shaving foam but there wasn't any, all he could find was a razor that Barbera used on her legs when she took a bath. Terry lathered his face with a bar of moisturising soap and shaved his face completely, just like Jenkins did every morning before work. When this laborious task was complete, he set to work on his hair. Terry's hair was curly and not really cut to any style, he found a tub of hair gel some of his kids used from time to time and worked a big dollop through his hair. He took a comb and gave himself a side parting going from right to left, Just like Jenkins.

"Not bad Jenkins, not bad at all, I could be you." He said smiling as he left the bathroom to get dressed, Barbera had already risen to make breakfast for the family.

It was a cold December morning, the 22nd of December to be precise. There was a thick layer of frost on the ground outside as Terry walked down the staircase to have breakfast with Barbera and the kids. Terry walked into the Kitchen and sat down at the head of the massive table. Barbera turned around from the sink and let out a loud, high-pitched shriek. Their youngest son, Rodney, the two-year-old who always had his high chair next to Terry's, began to cry and threw his bowl of Weetabix on the floor. The others were all staring at the new man at the head of the table with their mouths open in a state of shock, they'd never seen him clean shaven before.

"What the bloody hell have you done?" cried Barbera with a look of disgust on her face.

"Just fancied a change that's all Barb, no big deal." Terry said as he began slapping the upside down bottle of HP sauce over his plate of bacon and eggs.

"And what on earth have you done to your hair? You look like a right wally!" Said Barbera shaking her head in disbelief as she was bent down trying to clean up the mess Rodney had just made.

"Oh, leave it out why don't you Barb." Terry said, as he put a bit of toast into Rodney's mouth to calm him down.

Inside Terry's head he was so excited, but he knew he couldn't show it to anyone. He knew he had to play it cool otherwise Barbera would get suspicious and know he was up to something. The radical change in his appearance had upset everyone enough, so he continued to look pissed off with everyone's reaction and went back to eating his breakfast.

The kids, one by one, left the house for the last day of school before the Christmas holidays, some went by bus and the others were walking distance. Terry kissed Barbera goodbye as she was washing up the breakfast things in the sink. He said he'd be back home later than usual, as he had a little Christmas shopping to do on the way home from work. This didn't surprise Barbera one bit, like 98% of all men, they do their Christmas shopping at the very last minute. She didn't reply as she was still in a foul mood from the early morning antics.

Terry got in the car and drove off as per usual, except he didn't drive to the surgery for the last day of work before the holidays, he'd seen all the patients he had to the day before. Like I said previously, he didn't want Barbera to get suspicious, so he told a little white lie about going to work, and anyway, Terry had some serious shopping to do with his magic cheque book.

He parked the car in a large multi-level carpark in the middle of town; he knew he didn't want to park on the high street, just in case any more shops had had new security cameras installed like the Post office box place.

"First on the list I think" Terry said to himself as he glided down the street towards the hub of shops in the city centre.

"I'm gonna need some decent clothes If I'm to pull off the biggest cheque fraud / heist in history."

He was desperately in need of some new suits anyway, as all his other ones were getting pretty threadbare, the last time he bought a new suit was probably back in the late 70s, so not only were they falling apart but they looked pretty outdated.

There was an Austin Reed men's outfitters Terry knew of slap bang in the middle of town.

"Perfect." Terry said as he arrived at the front door. He had a quick scan to make sure there weren't any of those new CCTV cameras inside, there weren't, and inside the boutique he went.

"How may I be of assistance sir" a courteous voice said, coming from a slick little fellow who came scooting along to greet his first customer of the day. The salesman was impeccably dressed wearing a blue, pinstripe suit with a white shirt and a red, silk tie. His hair was jet black and slicked back just like Robert de Niro in his early films. Terry thought he could be Italian, but the name tag he wore on his Jacket said "Steve", so he thought otherwise.

"Jenkins is the name, Nigel Jenkins." said Terry in a rather pompous manner.

"A pleasure to meet you Mr Jenkins sir, I'm Steve, and what is it in particular we're after today sir?" said Steve with the utmost professionalism, his level of customer service was top-notch it has to be said.

"As you can see Steve, my suit is looking somewhat old-fashioned and tatty, I'm going to need at least three new ones, a new cashmere overcoat, some shirts and some new silk ties." Terry said in the manner of someone who is well off and knew exactly what he was talking about.

"Excellent Mr Jenkins sir, an extremely wise decision indeed if I may say so." Steve said as he was looking Terry up and down trying to gauge his measurements.

Steve guided Terry to the extensive range of suits that were hanging on the rails on the far side of the shop.

"Any preference as to the colour of the suits you require sir?" the salesman asked.

"Yes Steve, I'm thinking I'd like a blue pinstripe, dark blue double-breasted & a light grey three piece, like the one Sean Connery wears in Goldfinger." Terry replied in a rather smug manner.

"I like your style sir, may I be so bold as to say what impeccable taste you have sir." Said Steve holding his head high whilst holding his hands behind his back.

"Thank you Steve." Terry replied with a cheeky smile and a wink.

The Latin looking sales attendant hurried off towards the rail of suits that contained all the pinstripes in various colours, his fingers flicking through the suits like an expert vinyl collector in a record shop. He did the same in the double-breasted section and the three-piece suit area, in the space of a couple of minutes, Steve reappeared with the three suits Terry was after.

"The fitting room is just over there sir if you'd like to try them on." the salesman gestured, pointing to the corner of the room where there were three cubicles with red curtains pulled across them.

"Thank you Steve, and could you bring me a selection of your finest cotton shirts, lets say, half a dozen of various colours." Terry said as he trotted over to the fitting cubicle in the centre of the three that were on offer.

No sooner had Terry sat down on the little wooden, dark brown bench to take off his shoes, Steve was back to the cubicle and whispered through the curtain.

"I've just popped the shirts you requested on a little peg on the outside to your left sir, feel free to help yourself sir when you're ready." Said Steve in his usual courteous manner.

Terry reached out the side of the curtain to pick up the shirts and hung them on a peg inside the cubicle. One white, two blue (light & dark), one cream, and two paisley patterned shirts in different shades of red.

Terry finished taking off his old, scruffy suit he'd worn for years, removed the shirt he had on, and slipped into the new, crisp white shirt Steve had produced. It was a perfect fit, Steve was evidently a master of his craft, being able to size up a customer with a single glance was something Steve took enormous pride in.

The same with the blue pinstripe, as Terry looked at himself in the full-length mirror wearing the suit and shirt, he could see how well it fitted him, anyone would think it had been tailor made on Saville Row it looked that good.

Terry opened the curtain where Steve was waiting with his back to the cubicle, standing with his hands behind his back like a soldier standing at ease. Steve turned around with the grace of a ballet dancer and his face lit up with joy.

"That looks exquisite sir if I may say so, not too long in the sleeves for you sir?" Steve said as Terry held his arms out in front of him.

"No, it's a perfect fit Steve, you certainly are an expert in your field, you've definitely saved me a lot of time." Replied Terry sincerely.

"My pleasure sir, only too happy to be of service. Forgive me for asking sir, but what line of profession are you in?" Asked Steve delicately.

"I'm a bank manager Steve, it's pretty dull, but it pays well." Terry said casually as if he didn't really care too much about the line of work he was in.

"Ah I see sir, a very noble profession I must say, well, now you certainly look the part, you could be the chairman of The Bank of England with a suit like that." Said Steve as he was adjusting his crimson, silk tie.

"One day Steve, one day perhaps further down the line." Terry said as he was trying not to crack up laughing.

Terry walked back into the cubicle and sat down again to put his shoes back on, saying to Steve how he would like to keep on the new suit to go back to the office in. As Steve was collecting the shirts and suits that were hanging up inside the cubicle, Terry asked him to pick out for him a suitable black, cashmere overcoat and a dozen silk ties. Steve nodded his head efficiently and hurried off to collect the required items from their respective zones in the shop.

Terry put his old pair of black loafers on, gathered up his old suit that was lying on the floor and strolled over to the desk where Steve was already waiting for him. Terry transferred the contents of his old suit to the pockets on the new pinstripe he was wearing, then he asked the sales associate if he could kindly dispose of the shabby suit he no longer needed.

"Not a problem sir, I can take it to a charity shop for you on my way home tonight." replied Steve, as he took the old suit and placed.it underneath the counter out of sight.

Terry told Steve that he would take every item he had chosen for him and asked politely if he could tot up the bill.

"Certainly sir" replied Steve, as his fingers were punching the keys on the old-fashioned till. The speed of the man's fingers was a sight to behold, like a concert pianist, Terry thought to himself as he put his hand inside the interior pocket of the new suit jacket. Steve was nearly finished adding up the bill as Terry put the cheque book on the counter. Steve wrote the total cost of the garments on a piece of paper and slid it across the counter towards Terry, then he bagged up all the clothes for him at great speed. A hummingbird couldn't catch him at work.

Terry looked down at the piece of paper. His eyes widened when he saw the beautifully written, itemised bill, at the bottom was the grand total including tax. Two thousand, nine hundred and eighty-seven pounds and sixty-two pence.

"That's a silly number if ever I saw one." said Terry smiling, Steve took a slight step back as if he were afraid of some terrible, impending doom that was sure to be coming his way any second.

"Why don't we just round it up to three grand Steve? it's got a much better ring to it hasn't it my good man." said Terry as he wrote the first cheque in his brand new cheque book, making sure to sign it, "Nigel Jenkins."

"Of course sir of course." replied Steve with a sigh of relief. Terry handed the cheque to Steve, he gave it a quick glance and opened the till to place it carefully in one of the little compartments.

"Will there be anything else I can help you with today sir?" said Steve as he was tidying up all the coat-hangers that he'd just removed from the clothes Terry had purchased.

"As a matter-of-fact Steve there is, I'm going to need some new shoes to go with this fine suit." Terry said as he looked down at his old shoes, the left shoe even had a small hole in the sole which meant Terry's foot got wet every time it rained.

"Not a problem sir, there's a Russell & Bromley shoe shop not far from here, if you turn left out of here and walk down the street 50 yards or so you'll see it, you can't miss it." he said as he handed the collection of shiny, plastic Austin Reed bags to Terry over the counter.

Terry thanked him, took the bags and proceeded to walk out of the shop in the direction Steve had indicated. As Terry approached the door, Steve came running up alongside to hold the door open for him.

"Have an excellent day sir, I look forward to seeing you again." Steve said bowing his head ever so slightly.

"I'm sure you will Steve, thanks once again for your help and expertise, you truly are a master of your craft." replied Terry, clutching his shopping bags as he went outside onto the high street.

The high street was busier than before, as Terry walked the short distance to the shoe shop Steve had recommended earlier. Sure enough, there was precisely 50 yards between the two shops, Terry measured the distance with each pace he walked along the pavement. The electric doors slid open as Terry walked up to them, he got a blast of warm air down his neck as he passed through the doors.

Inside the shop there were a few customers browsing, but they didn't really look like they were going to make a purchase, Terry thought to himself. He scanned the ceiling of the shop and the corners for any sign of a surveillance system but there was nothing. Terry could see no one at the till, so he looked all round but could only see the three other customers inspecting some shoes on display. An old gentleman was sniffing a pair of brogues in such an odd way, Terry thought he was getting some sort kick out of it.

"Whatever floats yer boat." Terry mumbled under his breath.

"Can I help you sir?" a voice called out behind Terry.

Terry turned back around towards the till that had been previously unoccupied and did a double take, he couldn't believe what he saw in front of him.

"Steve! what the dickens are you doing in here?" Exclaimed Terry with a very puzzled look on his face.

"Ah, I see sir, judging by the Austin Reed bags you're holding, I'd wager a pretty penny you've recently acquired some fine tailoring where my twin brother works."

"Well, I'll be damned!, twins working on the same high street fifty yards apart, extraordinary!" replied Terry a little less confused than before.

"My names Victor, Steves identical twin brother." Said the carbon copy of the previous sales agent.

It was uncanny, normally with identical twins there is often a very slight difference, perhaps a mole on the face that's different to the other sibling or something like that, but these two were completely identical in every way. Terry even noticed that Victor was wearing exactly the same three piece, blue suit, the same crimson silk tie with a white shirt as his brother. Even the haircut was the same and the shoes as well, Terry noticed.

"I'm Jenkins, Nigel Jenkins." Terry said as he tried his best to sound like a bank manager in his new pinstripe.

"Pleased to make your acquaintance Mr Jenkins sir, I assume you need some good quality footwear to go with the fine suits my brother has provided." Said Victor looking down at the tired, old pair of loafers Terry had on. Victor was shaking his head from side to side and began sucking air in through his teeth like a car mechanic inspecting a broken down vehicle.

"Oxfords or brogues sir?" said Victor efficiently, still looking down at Terry's shoes. In his head he knew exactly which size was required, like his twin brother, he never needed to take actual measurements.

"Oxfords please, a brown pair and I need a black pair for going to the Freemasons meetings." replied Terry.

"Not a problem sir, If you'd like to take a seat over there I'll be with you in two shakes of a lamb's tail." Said Victor, as he walked briskly around the counter showing the seating area to Terry.

The fastidious sales agent breezed passed his customer and picked up two pairs of shoes from one of the display tables in the middle of the room. He walked back to his customer and crouched down in front of him, gesturing to the old shoes Terry was wearing.

"May I sir?" said Victor.

"Certainly my good man." replied Terry.

Victor removed the shoes and as he inspected them, he raised the left shoe up and poked his forefinger through the hole and wiggled it a bit.

"You really ought to have come to see me earlier sir if I may say so." said Victor raising his eyebrows.

"Your're right Victor, but you see, I'm a bank manager and I like to get my money's worth." said Terry.

"I quite understand sir, but with the very greatest of respect, and you can shoot me down in flames if I'm wrong. One must never try to save money when it comes to purchasing a pair of shoes or a new bed, because if you're not in one, you're in the other, you see." said the sales agent as he was slipping on the new pair of brown oxfords onto Terry's feet.

"How very true Victor, I'd never thought of it like that before." Said Terry, with a look like someone who has just gained a terribly important fact that could save lives the world over.

Victor tied the laces and asked Terry to have a little walk around making sure the size and comfort was suitable, still in the crouched position and looking hard at the shoes as Terry took a few strides.

"They're perfect, very comfortable, how did you know my size?" Terry said in disbelief as he was gliding around the shop floor.

"Tricks of the trade sir, tricks of the trade." said Victor as he stood up with a cheeky smile and a wink.

"I'll keep this pair on to wear back to the office, if you could bag up the black pair for me and dispose of the old pair I'd be most grateful." Said Terry, as he was looking at his new shoes in the low level mirror on the wall feeling very pleased with himself.

"Certainly sir not a problem, If you'd like to come over to the till." Said Victor, as he gathered up the two pairs of shoes on the floor and the respective shoe-boxes.

The two men walked back over to the till and Terry reached inside his jacket pocket for his cheque book. Victor placed the worn-out pair of shoes underneath the counter and bagged up the other pair. Victor tapped the keys on the cash register in exactly the same manner as his twin brother had done previously.

"Right then sir, that'll be six hundred and forty pounds all together." Said Victor clasping his hands together in front of him.

"Perfect." replied Terry as he wrote his second cheque. Terry then handed over the cheque and Victor gave it a cursory glance before placing into the drawer of the till. Terry glanced through the large, plate-glass window of the shop and could see that it was just starting to snow a little, the snowflakes dancing in the wind like tiny, white fireflies. Terry bent down and removed the new cashmere coat he'd recently purchased from Victor's brother.

"Let me help you sir." Said Victor, as he ran around the other side of the counter and helped Terry into his sumptuous, new overcoat.

"The perfect accoutrement for such a cold day like today sir." said Victor looking out the window.

"Thank you, Victor you've been a great help." said Terry as he picked up his shopping bags. Victor handed him the new shopping bag with the second pair of new shoes and the empty box for the new pair he was already wearing, and walked over to the door. As Terry approached the door, Victor bowed his head slightly and wished Terry a good day and a merry Christmas.

"Same to you Victor, see you next time." Terry said, as he walked through the automatic doors back onto the high street where the snow was settling on the cold, grey pavement.

As Terry stood outside the shoe shop, he put down the bags he was holding in his left hand to check what time it was.

"Ten o'clock, I must crack on." He said softly, he raised his wrist again and looked at the watch. It was an old, Casio digital with a plastic strap that was showing its age.

"I could really do with something fancier." Terry thought to himself, as he lowered his arm to pick up the shopping bags he'd carefully set down on the snow covered pavement.

He started off walking again in the same direction as before, and could see there was a Jeweller's shop not far away on the same side of the street.

As Terry approached the entrance to the shop, a white van pulled up right in front of the establishment. He looked at the writing on the side of the van which read "Falcon Security Service."

"It's the same one that I saw outside the P.O. box place." Terry said to himself, as he walked through the door to the premises. Inside the shop, Terry walked up to a display cabinet and analysed the various timepieces on offer. Through the reflection in the glass he could see the door behind him swing open and in walked two workmen, wearing brown overalls and flat caps. They were both carrying step ladders and had leather, builders style work belts containing screwdrivers and tape measures. Terry looked up at the corners of the ceiling that were devoid of any surveillance apparatus. He knew he had to be quick this time, unlike the previous two boutiques he had visited.

"Can I help you sir?" came a softly spoken voice from behind the counter on one side of the room. The jeweller approached the well-dressed gentleman with a plethora of shopping bags on the floor either side of him.

"Yes, I think you just might be able to Mr…" said Terry to the equally, well dressed, grey haired old man.

"Cohen, Abraham Cohen is my name sir, and you are?" the elderly, well-spoken gentleman said.

"Jenkins, Nigel Jenkins, pleased to meet you Mr Cohen." said Terry, as he thrust his hand forward to shake hands. After the quick, but firm handshake, Terry raised his left arm to show Mr Cohen the horrible, Japanese watch he was wearing. The look of horror on the jewellers face was priceless, evidently one thing he despised was digital wristwatches.

"Dear oh dear, that simply won't do at all sir, I'd better find you something more appropriate." Said Mr Cohen genuinely concerned. At the same time, Terry could see the two workmen erecting their stepladders in two corners of the front the shop.

"I think I already know what I want." said Terry, pointing to the glass display cabinet directly in front of him. Mr Cohen unlocked the front of the cabinet with a small, brass key he produced from his trouser pocket that was attached to his belt via a lengthy silver chain.

Terry pointed to the watch he wanted and Mr Cohen reached inside and handed it to him.

"The Omega Speedmaster sir, it's the watch that the Americans used during the Apollo space missions, the first ever wristwatch to be used on the surface of the moon, tried and tested to work in zero gravity." Said a very proud Mr Cohen. He took great pride in knowing every minuscule detail about the chronographs he sold.

"It's exquisite" Terry said, inspecting the elegant timepiece. He loved the way the second hand swept around the face in a smooth fashion, unlike cheap watches that tick along. It felt a lot heavier compared to the old Casio he was wearing.

"Isn't it just sir, I've always admired Omegas, elegant & functional without being over the top like the Rolexs over there." Mr Cohen said pointing to another display case to the rear of the shop. Terry nodded his head and checked the price that was written in tiny, but beautifully hand written script on the empty space inside the display cabinet the watch had sat in.

"Three and a half does that say Mr Cohen?" Terry said trying not to sound afraid of the price, as if he were talking about the price of potatoes with a market trader.

"That's right sir, three thousand five hundred pounds, worth every penny, pure quality & fine craftsmanship comes at price." Replied Mr Cohen confidently.

"It most certainly does Mr Cohen, I'd like to try it on if I may." Said Terry as he removed his Casio and put it into his trouser pocket.

"Of course sir, not a problem." Replied Mr Cohen, as he placed the watch on Terry's outstretched left arm. The silver chain-link bracelet was a bit too big for Terry's wrist but boy did it look fantastic.

"I love it!, I'll take it." Said Terry smiling. Mr Cohen inspected the gap between the bracelet and Terry's wrist and said "It needs two links taking out sir, if you'd like to follow me over to the counter over there." Mr Cohen led the way and went behind the counter to open one of the many drawers. Terry removed the Omega and carefully placed it on the counter in front of Mr Cohen. The jeweller produced a small leather pouch and opened it on the counter, inside were a dozen special watchmakers screwdrivers. He took one of the smallest ones out and began the process of removing two links from the shiny bracelet, one each side of the fastening mechanism. Within a few seconds the job was complete, and he handed the watch back to Terry to put back on his wrist.

"Perfect, fits like a glove Mr Cohen." Terry said as he reached into his jacket pocket to remove his chequebook. As Terry started writing out the cheque, there was a loud bang behind him which made him jump. One of the workmen had dropped one of the large reels of cable onto the floor, narrowly missing a display case containing a vast array of diamond engagement rings.

"Careful you bloody fools!, I'm paying you to put up security cameras, not to destroy my display cases!" Mr Cohen yelled out, as Terry handed him the cheque.

"I'd love to stay and chat about watches with you Mr Cohen but I'm afraid I really must dash back to the bank, I've got an awful lot of work on at the moment, busy time of year you see." Terry said looking at the new watch on his wrist.

"I quite understand sir, maybe next time you're in town." Mr Cohen said as he placed the cheque in the till and handed Terry the small bag containing the empty watch box and receipt.

"Yes, of course." Terry said as he gathered up his shopping bags and started walking to the front door with Mr Cohen following.

"A pleasure doing business with you sir and I hope to see you again." Said Mr Cohen as he opened the door in front of Terry.

"Thank you Mr Cohen, you've been most helpful, goodbye & god bless." Said Terry as he turned and walked out the door. The door shut behind him and as Terry began walking, he could hear Mr Cohen yelling out Yiddish swearwords at the two men working on top of the stepladders. Terry grinned as he walked back in the other direction to put all his shopping bags into the boot of the red Volvo waiting in the car park.

With the morning's shopping placed neatly in the car's boot and covered with an old picnic blanket, the well dressed Terry walked back to the row of shops with a spring in his step. He now needed to buy presents for Barbera and the kids, perfume & cosmetics for Barbera and the five elder daughters, and the new Sega mega-drive computer games console for the two youngest boys. Terry was hoping this wouldn't take too long as he hated shopping normally, especially with his own money, but today was different.

After walking for a short space of time, Terry arrived outside one of the town centres perfume & cosmetics shops and looked up at the beautiful hand written pink signage above the large window. The sign read "Southwest Perfumery & Beauty." He walked though the door and into the warm boutique, he was happy to be out of the cold high street, the snow was falling harder than before. Terry walked straight up to the counter as he wanted to be in and out as quick as possible. Behind the counter stood two young women, both with bleached blonde hair and both wearing an enormous quantity of makeup & very strong perfume. It looked like they'd applied the foundation makeup with a builder's trowel, it looked half an inch thick in some places.

"Morning sir, can we help?" said the two girls in unison, they both had very strong Plymouth accents which Terry always found amusing.

"Morning girls, I need to buy some presents for my wife & five daughters." Terry said smiling, leaning his right elbow on the counter in front of him.

"Perfume or makeup sir?" said the taller of the two sales assistants.

"Both, my wife likes Chanel no. 5, and if you could help me choose something suitable for my teenage daughters I'd be most grateful."

Both the sales assistants faces lit up, they knew this would be a hefty bill. The majority of male customers only ever bought one bottle of perfume at a time for their wives or girlfriends, on the odd occasion both, but their latest customer wanted to buy 6 bottles and makeup!

The two women turned around and removed several, different coloured and interestingly shaped bottles of perfume and placed them on the counter in front of Terry. He looked down and saw the familiar bottle of Chanel no. 5, and five other bottles, some he'd never seen before but all very well-known French brands, ranging from Dior to Yves Saint Laurent.

"Perfect, and could you perhaps find me some suitable cosmetics for my wife and daughters, matching brands to go with each type of perfume, like those boxes on display over there." Terry said pointing to the display stand on the other side of the room with a big red and gold sign hanging from the ceiling that read, "Christmas Ideas."

"Right you are sir." said the shorter of the two shop assistants, as she hurriedly glided over to the cosmetics display and collected the items Terry requested.

"Anything else today sir?" said the tall girl behind the counter, as the shorter of the two returned, carrying all six boxes of makeup piled high in front of her large, low cut cleavage.

"That's it for today thank you." Terry said as he swiftly removed his chequebook, the shorter, older shop assistant began tapping the keys on the cash register with her long, bright pink nails.

Terry suddenly remembered, he hadn't checked to see if there were any CCTV cameras when he walked into the boutique earlier. He glanced up above the two assistants heads, to check the ceiling corners behind them, and then he turned around a full three hundred and sixty degrees, scanning the ceiling for surveillance cameras, there were none. When he turned back around the face the women, he started patting down his pockets in an effort to look like he'd lost something.

"Terribly sorry girls, but I appear to have left my pen back at my office in the bank." Terry said looking a bit flustered, not because of a forgotten pen, but because he hadn't checked for CCTV cameras when he entered the shop.

"Not to worry sir, you can use mine, I imagine you've got a lot of work on at the moment what with it being Christmas an' all, that's probably why you forgot to bring your pen with you isn't it?" Said the tall one, as the older, shorter sales assistant piped up "Yeah, everyone out spending money they havn't got int' it like."

"Yes, quite so." Said Terry, as he took the blue, ballpoint pen from the shop assistants perfume smelling hand.

"So that's a grand total of four hundred and eighty-five pounds and fifty pence sir." said the shorter of the two smiling at Terry.

"Thanks girls you've been most helpful." Terry said as he filled out the cheque and handed it over. The shorter one looked at the cheque briefly and looked back up to Terry and said "Thank you Mr Jenkins, I hope the girls like their presents, they're very lucky to have such a wonderful dad who spoils them so much."

"Yes, they're little angels, love em' to bits I really do." Terry said smirking, as the shop assistant put the cheque in the cash register.

Terry wished the two sales assistants a merry Christmas and walked out of the shop. It had just stopped snowing, but it was still bitterly cold outside, with a good inch of snow on the pavement with the cars and busses turning the snow on the road into brown slush.

All Terry needed to buy now was the computer games console for his two youngest sons. There were two computer shops in town he knew of, "Computer Zone" & "Computer World". He always used the shop "Computer Zone" for his own personal needs, as the owner was a fellow Freemason who always gave Terry a good discount for paying with cash; therefore, Terry started walking towards "Computer World", because of the nature of this particular days preferred method of payment.

The door to the computer shop swung open and in walked Terry bringing with him a blast of cold air. The shop was empty, apart from two young lads who looked like they were probably sixteen or seventeen, and the shopkeeper behind the counter. The two lads were at the far end of the shop playing on a demo version of a computer game that was on display, the shopkeeper was behind the counter at the front of the shop going through a huge pile of paperwork he had in front of him. Terry approached the counter and said, "I was wondering if you could help me, my boys want the new Sega megadrive console for Christmas…"

"I'm terribly sorry, but I've only got one left, it's my demonstration version over there." The shopkeeper pointed to the two young lads who were deeply engrossed at the far end of the shop.

"If you could let me have it anyway, I'd make it worth your while sir, I really must have it, I can't disappoint my boys at Christmas you see." said Terry, putting both hands together like the way Indian people greet each other.

The shopkeeper looked up from his paperwork at Terry, squinting over the top of his half-moon spectacles. He analysed the customer in front of him for a couple of seconds, and judging by his attire, he could see he was a gentleman of means.

"Make it worth my while eh, hows that then?" Said the shopkeeper, cocking his head to one side as he spoke.

"Yes of course sir, I'll pay you fifty pounds extra for the machine and if you could pick out ten of the best games for me I think that should make you happy, my boys too." said Terry, still holding his hands in the praying position in front of him.

The shopkeepers demeanour changed completely, and he removed his reading glasses and placed them on the counter. He then walked around the counter and headed over to the two lads at the far end of the shop, as he did this Terry did his usual security check of the corners of the ceiling, no cameras were visible. Terry remained at the counter and placed his chequebook on the glass top, casually looking at various computer parts that were on display inside.

"Oi you two!, clear off, it's been sold." Yelled the shopkeeper at the two youths.

The two lads immediately put down the game controllers and began making their way towards the door, as they passed Terry they gave him an evil look, they weren't happy.

The shopkeeper packed the machine back into its box with the connecting cables and the two controllers, then he walked over to the shelf of games and picked out the top ten bestsellers. Then he made his way back behind the counter with the console and the stack of ten games in his hands.

"Anything else sir?" beamed the shopkeeper as he was adding up the bill on the cash register.

"That'll be all for today, I really must dash back to my office at the bank." said Terry, as he picked up the pen that was lying on the counter.

"Right then sir, so that's fifty quid extra for the console, which comes to three hundred, and the games are thirty quid a pop. Making a grand total of six hundred all together, please." Said the shopkeeper, grinning from ear to ear.

Terry filled out the cheque and slid it across the counter putting down the pen he'd used next to it. The shopkeeper put his glasses back on and picked up the cheque and held it close to his face.

"Right then Mr… Jenkins, hope to see you again." as he then placed the cheque in the cash register.

"Oh, I'm sure you will, you've been most helpful." Said Terry, as he picked up the two bags the shopkeeper had prepared for him.

"A very merry Christmas to you and the family sir, that little lot should keep the boys busy over the holidays." Said the shopkeeper, with a wink and still grinning.

"I'm sure it will, merry Christmas to you too." Said Terry, as he turned around and walked out of the shop back onto the high street.

A snow flurry had started again as Terry was walking back to the car park, he looked at his new watch and could see it was just after midday.

"Getting a bit peckish now, back home for some beans on toast and a snooze in front of the fire I reckon." Terry thought to himself, as he approached the awaiting red Volvo. He opened the boot of the estate car and placed the two bags he had in his right hand with the others and replaced the picnic blanket as he had done before. He shut the boot gently (he hated it when people slam car doors and boots, completely unnecessary) and got into the driver's seat and turned the ignition key. The big Swedish brick of a car roared into life and kicked out a big cloud of black smoke as it always did. He turned on the radio and tuned into BBC Radio 2. He was a big fan of the DJ Steve Wright and the song currently being played was one of Terry's personal favourites, one of Abbas many hit songs, "Money, Money, Money,."

Chapter 5 : The demise of Jenkins

Terry arrived back at the house at half-past twelve, he drove past the space with no snow on the road where Barbera always parked her car, and reversed his back into the driveway in front of the garage door. Terry got out of the car and walked around to the rear to open the garage door, he turned the key and opened the sideways sliding door just wide enough for him to fit through. He turned back to the car to open the boot and collected all the shopping bags that were inside. He placed the shopping bags neatly under one of the workbenches inside the garage, apart from the ones containing his new clothes and shoes, those he took back to the house after locking the garage door behind him.

Terry knew the house would be empty as Barbera was probably out doing some last minute Christmas food shopping and all the kids were still at school. He went upstairs to hang up his new suits and shirts in the wardrobe in the master bedroom, the dozen silk ties he rolled up and placed deep in his sock drawer. He changed out of the new suit he was wearing and put on his normal home attire, a pair of old jeans, plain white t-shirt and a green, v-neck pullover. Terry then went into the bathroom and rinsed his hair in the sink to get all the hair gel out, he hated the stuff. After towelling his head vigorously, he looked at himself in the mirror above the sink. "Much better Terry," he said to himself aloud, his hair was back to normal, curly and no side parting. He also noticed that he already had a very fine amount of greyish stubble beginning to form since shaving at seven o'clock earlier that morning.

Terry was in the kitchen at the breakfast table finishing off his plate of baked beans on toast, mopping up the plate with an extra slice of bread. He heard the front door open and into the kitchen walked Barbera carrying an enormous turkey, it almost looked like it was too big to fit in the oven.

"What are you doing?" said Barbera, with a look of complete shock on her face as she set the massive bird on the kitchen table in front of Terry.

"I'm eating my sodding lunch, what does it look like I'm doing?" Said Terry in a defensive manner as he stood up to put his plate and cutlery in the dishwasher.

"You said this morning you were going to be home late after work." Said Barbera, as she opened the fridge wondering how she was going to make room for the turkey.

"Yeah well, my afternoon appointments phoned up to cancel because of the snow. I gave Tanya & Judy (Terry's two dental nurses) the afternoon off and did my shopping on the way home, did all my shopping in half an hour." Terry said with a smug grin.

"I see you've washed that gel out of your hair then." Barbera said still looking at the open refrigerator and scratching her head.

"Yeah, didn't suit me." Terry said, as he made his way out of the kitchen to go and light the fire in the lounge. Once Terry made sure the fire was well lit, he put three big logs on and retired to the sofa. He pushed two cushions to one end to rest his head on and laid down in the foetal position, it only took him a couple of minutes to drift off into a deep sleep. It had been a very busy morning.

Christmas and the New Year festivities came and went, and what a brilliant festive period it was for Terry and his family. Barbera and the kids couldn't believe how lucky they were, spoiled rotten with the best presents they'd ever received. Terry got the usual seven pairs of novelty socks and Christmas woollen jumper but he didn't mind, he'd done alright for himself he thought, as he looked at the time on his fancy new watch. He told Barbera he only paid sixty pounds for it; she had no idea what a real watch costs.

The second week in January, both Terry and I went back to work on the Monday. I didn't see a single customer all day in the antiques shop, not that it bothered me, it gave me the perfect opportunity to read one of the many books I got for Christmas. By mid afternoon as I was performing the daily ritual of dusting off some of the larger pieces of furniture. I decided to phone the dental surgery to see if Terry fancied having a beer with me after work. Judy picked up the phone and said Terry couldn't come to the phone right now as he was busy doing a root canal procedure, but he should be able to finish work at five o'clock.

"Ok Judy, thanks, tell him I'll meet down there cos' I'm gonna knock off in a bit as it's so quiet." I said, as I was putting my duster back in the old Edwardian desk I used in the shop.

"I'll pass on the message for you Rob, bye bye." Said Judy, as she hung up the phone.

I was dying to get down the pub for a pint; I hadn't touched a drop during the first week of January as I had probably overdone it during Christmas and New Year's eve, but you can't stay on the wagon forever.

I walked into the bar of the Dog & Duck and ordered a Pint of ice cold lager, I had a terrible thirst on and needed a refreshing drink. Sally pulled a pint of the amber nectar and set it down on the bar in front of me, I took a big slurp and carried it over to my favourite table with a copy of the Times newspaper I found lying on the bar. After an hour had passed and I was on to the back pages of the paper, I heard the door open, a cold blast of air came rushing in which made me turn my head to look back towards the bar. There were three red faced, retired farmers sitting at the far end of the bar drinking Pints of cloudy cider, I couldn't see the other end of the bar as it was obscured by one of the many, thick wooden, floor to ceiling posts in the pub. I turned my head back towards my table to finish reading my paper.

"Happy New Year Rob, have a good Christmas?" Terry said, standing in front of the roaring log fire taking a sip of a pint of Guinness.

I lowered the newspaper to see Terry standing there wearing a beautiful, three piece, light grey suit, white cotton shirt with a navy blue silk tie. I looked down at his brand new, shiny black shoes.

"I've been expecting you Mr Bond, take a seat you flash bugger." I said, as I sat back in my chair rocking it back and forth on its back legs trying to do my best Bond villain impression.

"You like my new suit then? Moneypenny." Said Terry as he sat down and placed his glass on one of the cardboard beer mats that were already on the table.

"I love it Terry, classy stuff." I said, taking another sip of lager.

Terry rested his forearms on the table and as the jacket and shirt sleeves retracted a bit towards the elbows, I noticed the sparkling Omega chronograph on his wrist.

"So tell me James, when are you going to take me out for dinner?, you can't make me wait forever." I said using my best Moneypenny voice.

"No seriously Terry, what's going on?, have you inherited some money or something?" I said using my normal voice.

"Theres a funny story about that actually Rob," said Terry, as he had a quick look around the pub making sure none of the other patrons could hear our conversation. We both leant in closer to each other as Terry began to speak quieter than he normally did. Over the course of the next hour, Terry recounted all the details of his plan to get back at Jenkins from A to Z. The P.O. box he'd set up, the fake, provisional driving license, the magic chequebook, all using the bank managers name, date of birth and National Insurance number. He also went into great detail about the spending spree he had, in the space of a morning's shopping Terry had spent seven thousand, two hundred and twenty-five pounds and fifty pence.

"My god Terry, you're a bloody genius!" I exclaimed as I nearly fell backwards off my chair.

"But what about Jenkins?, he could get in a load of shit for that couldn't he?" I said, a little concerned.

"Nah, when I was out shopping he was probably at work in his office wasn't he, so he'll have all the bank staff as witnesses to back up his alibi." Said Terry looking completely unphased by the whole thing.

"Yeah, you're probably right Terry, no harm done hey, no body, no crime." I replied, taking the last sip of my pint.

"That's quite a cunning stunt you've pulled I must say old boy, deserves another pint I reckon, I'll get this round." I said, as I made my way back to the bar with Terry leaning casually back in his chair, with his hands behind his head looking very pleased with himself.

The week after, we were both back in the routine of going to work and having lunch in the pub every other day. We didn't even mention the shopping spree when we were chatting; it was almost like we'd both forgotten all about it. On the Friday after work, Terry went into the bank to pay in some cheques that patients had paid him with. As Terry approached the bank he saw two police cars parked right outside the front door, they looked like they'd been abandoned as the drivers and passenger doors had been left wide open. Terry walked into the bank, briefcase in one hand and stroking his short beard with the other. He walked up to the cashier's desk and opened his briefcase on the counter in front of the glass partition. Up on the second floor you could see the windows to the offices, Terry could see four police officers through the window inside Jenkins's office.

"Hi Margaret how are you?" said Terry as he took out the cheques he had in his briefcase and slid them into the revolving drawer on the counter.

"Fine thanks Terry," she said as the drawer spun around so she could remove the cheques on her side.

"What's going on up there?" said Terry pointing his thumb up to the manager's office.

"You'll never believe this Terry, turns out that Nigel has been defrauding the bank, he ripped off over seven grand just before Christmas! Not only that, he did it all in his own name the bloody idiot." said Margaret thumbing through the stack of cheques Terry had given her.

"How can they prove it was really him?, surely he must have an alibi." said Terry trying not to look too concerned.

"Well you see Terry, all the fake cheques he wrote were on the 22nd of December, he wasn't at work that day because he'd booked the day off to go fishing, well, that's his version anyway, except he's got no witnesses to back up his story." Said Margaret as she placed the cheques in the till.

Terry looked back up towards the office to see the door swing open, out came the four police officers with Jenkins handcuffed to the second officer. Down the spiral staircase they came, with Jenkins sobbing uncontrollably like a little schoolgirl, holding his head low. The boys in blue quickly escorted the criminal out of the bank, he was crying all the way to the awaiting police cars outside on the pavement.

Terry turned back to the cashier's desk, slapped shut the briefcase and took it by the handle.

"Well well Margaret, bank managers eh, you just can't trust them these days can you, fat cats the lot of them with their faces in the trough." said Terry as he slid the briefcase off the counter.

"I never liked him Terry, to tell you the truth, I always thought he was a slimy bugger." said Margaret, with an air of defiance in her east London accent.

"I couldn't agree more, anyway, see you next Friday, say hi to the family for me." said Terry winking.

"Will do Terry, give my love to Barb and the kids, mind how you go, be lucky." said Margaret, as she got up from her desk to make herself a cup of tea.

Terry turned around and walked towards the main entrance. As he passed one of the offices on the ground floor, he could faintly hear music coming from a radio inside, as he got closer, he could hear the opening bars to another one of his favourite songs. It was another of Abbas greatest hits, "The winner takes it all."